Driving my Tractor

Written by **Jan Dobbins**   Illustrated by **David Sim**   Sung by **SteveSongs**

Barefoot Books
Step inside a story

Driving my tractor down a bumpy road,

And in my trailer, there's a heavy load.

There's a black-and-white cow
Going moo, moo, moo!
It's a very busy day.

Chug, chug,
Clank, clank, toot!

It's a very busy day.

Driving my tractor down a bumpy road,

And in my trailer, there's a heavy load.

There are two gray donkeys
Going eeyore, eeyore!
It's a very busy day.

Chug, chug,
Clank, clank, toot!

It's a very busy day.

Driving my tractor down a bumpy road,

And in my trailer, there's a heavy load.

There are three pink pigs
Going oink, oink, oink!

It's a very
busy day.

Chug, chug,
Clank, clank, toot!
It's a very busy day.

Driving my tractor down a bumpy road,

And in my trailer, there's a heavy load.

There are four white lambs
Going mah, mah, mah!
It's a very busy day.

Driving my tractor down a bumpy road,

And in my trailer, there's a heavy load.

There are five brown chickens
Going cluck, cluck, cluck!
It's a very busy day.

Chug, chug,
Clank, clank, toot!

It's a very busy day.

Driving my tractor down a bumpy road,
The trailer hit a stone and it shook my load.

The animals fell out, and they ran away!

It's a very busy day.

Driving my tractor back home again,
Chugging along down the bumpy lane,

Farmers have lots of different machines to help them with their work.

Trailers carry foodstuffs, animals and other equipment.

Tractors tow heavy equipment, such as trailers and plows.

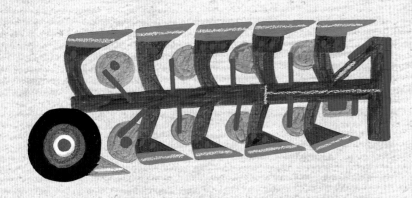

Plows turn the soil to make it ready for sowing seeds.

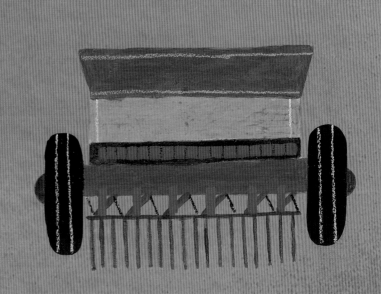

Seed drills plant seeds deep in the soil.

Combine harvesters cut wheat, oats and barley and separate the grain from the stems.

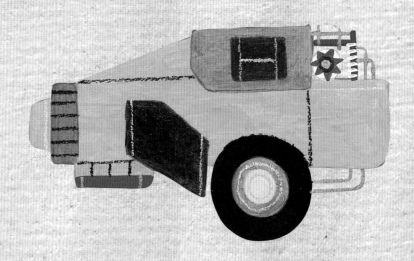

Balers gather harvested grain stems or mown grass and make them into bales of straw or hay.

Trucks transport smaller items than trailers and are designed to move easily across rough ground.

Milk trucks take milk from dairy farms to factories.

These are some of the crops that farmers grow.

Potatoes and sweet potatoes are sown in spring and are ready to be harvested when they have flowered.

Carrots are grown from seeds. They can be cultivated nearly all year round.

Sunflowers can be grow during the summer.

Beetroot is sown in spring and harvested from summer to autumn.

Onions and leeks are planted in spring, and are usually ready to eat by midsummer.

Wheat, barley and oats are cereal crops. They are usually sown in spring and harvested during late summer.

Squash and pumpkins are sown in late spring or early summer. They can be picked when quite young, or left to grow larger.

Sweet corn is a cereal crop. It is sown in spring.

Cabbages, cauliflower and turnips are usually sown in spring and harvested in summer or autumn. Cabbages are also grown in winter.

Driving my Tractor

Barefoot Books, 2067 Massachusetts Ave, Cambridge, MA 02140

Text and composition copyright © 2009 by Jan Dobbins
and Starshine Music Ltd
Illustrations copyright © 2009 by David Sim
The moral rights of Jan Dobbins and David Sim have been asserted
Lead vocals by SteveSongs
SteveSongs appears courtesy of PBSKids
Music arrangement copyright © 2009 by Mark Collins,
NewSense Music Productions
Recorded, mixed and mastered by Real World Studios, England
Animation by KZ Films, New York

First published in the United States of America
by Barefoot Books, Inc in 2009
This paperback edition first published in 2011
All rights reserved

Reproduction by B & P International, Hong Kong
Printed in China on 100% acid-free paper

This book was typeset in Slappy and Take-out-the-garbage
The illustrations were prepared in acrylics and pastels

British Cataloguing-in-Publication Data:
a catalogue record for this book is available
from the British Library

ISBN 978-1-84686-664-7

SteveSongs - lead vocals
Mark Collins - Musical director and
arranger, piano and bass
Ben Waghorn - piccolo and tenor sax
Dave Ford - trumpet
Kevin O'Rourke - Drums

11